P9-CCO-828

The
GOLDEN GOOSE

COLLECTED BY THE BROTHERS GRIMM

retold and illustrated by

Dennis McDermott

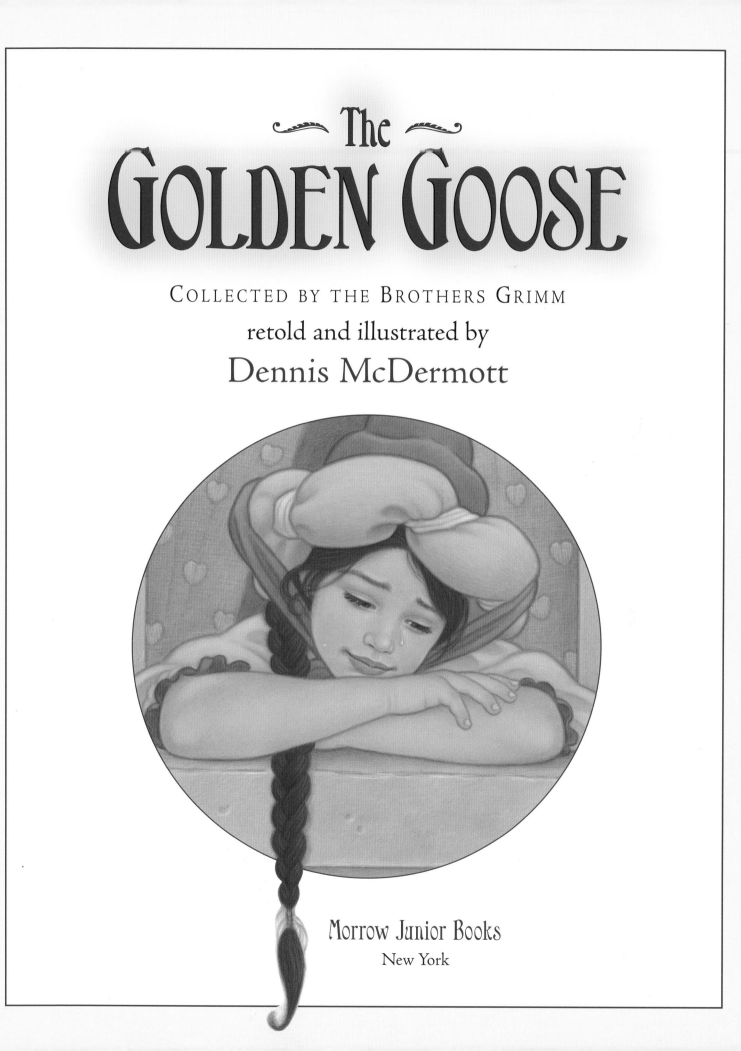

Morrow Junior Books

New York

Acrylic and pencil were used for the full-color illustrations.
The text type is 16-point Jenson.
Copyright © 2000 by Dennis McDermott

All rights reserved. No part of this book may be reproduced or utilized
in any form or by any means, electronic or mechanical, including
photocopying, recording, or by any information storage and retrieval
system, without permission in writing from the Publisher.

Published by Morrow Junior Books
a division of William Morrow and Company, Inc.
1350 Avenue of the Americas, New York, NY 10019
www.williammorrow.com

Printed in Hong Kong by South China Printing Company (1988) Ltd.

10 9 8 7 6 5 4 3 2 1

Library of Congress Cataloging-in-Publication Data
McDermott, Dennis.
The golden goose/by the Brothers Grimm; retold and illustrated by Dennis
McDermott.
p. cm.
Summary: Hans's generosity helps him gain a princess for his bride.
ISBN 0-688-11402-4 (trade)—ISBN 0-688-11403-2 (library)
[1. Fairy tales.   2. Folklore—Germany.]   I. Grimm, Jacob, 1785–1863.
II. Grimm, Wilhelm, 1786–1859.   III. Goldene Gans. English.
IV. Title.   PZ8.M1743Go 2000   398.2'0943'02—dc21   [E]   99-34513   CIP

WITHDRAWN

C. 1

PUBLIC LIBRARY

J 398.43
M134 g

FOR THE
GOLDEN GOOSE
KIDS

Long ago there lived a poor woodsman who had three sons. One day the oldest son, Pieter, told his father that he planned to chop down the biggest tree in the forest.

"The king will hear of my strength," Pieter boasted, "and reward me with a place in his service!"

"It's a good plan," said his father. "But when you go, remember to be kind to those you meet."

Pieter took a pancake and a flask of cider, and shouldering his ax, he strode into the forest.

By and by the boy came to a huge old tree. "This will do," he decided, and sat down to enjoy his lunch first.

Just then a little troll popped out of the bushes and said, "Please give me a bite of your pancake and a sip of your cider. . . . I'm *so* hungry and thirsty."

"Who are you?" asked Pieter.

"Someone who knows a secret about this tree," said the troll. "I'll tell you for a bite of your lunch."

Pieter frowned. "I already know all there is to know about trees. And I can't share my lunch with you—there isn't enough."

"Just a crumb of pancake and a thimbleful of cider," begged the troll. "I can help you."

"How can someone so small help me?" Pieter laughed.

And the troll went away.

Pieter gobbled his lunch. Then he grabbed his ax and swung at the giant tree. *Thwump!*

The tree's thick bark was barely scratched.

Maybe this won't be so easy, the boy thought, and he swung again with all his might. *Thrack!*

Suddenly the ax broke in two. Its iron top flew into the air and came down hard on Pieter's noggin.

"Ouch!" he yelled. And poor Pieter went home with a bump on his head as big as a hen's egg.

Next morning the second brother, Dieter, said he wanted to try his luck at the giant tree. "I'll succeed where Pieter failed!" he bragged.

"Ah, me . . . ," sighed the woodsman. But he wished his son well, only warning him to be kind to those he met.

In a while Dieter came to the tree. "This won't be hard," said the boy. "But first I'll eat lunch."

No sooner did he open his pouch than the same little troll appeared, asking for a bite of his food. Dieter refused as rudely as his brother.

"I can't share my lunch with every hungry troll who comes along!" he complained, and the troll went away.

Can you guess what happened next? *Thwump! Thrack!* And Dieter went home with a bump on his head, just as Pieter had.

Now, the youngest son of the woodsman was a kindhearted boy named Hans. His father loved him dearly but thought he daydreamed too much.

"Hans," said the father, "don't you wish to earn a place in the king's service as your brothers do?"

"My place here suits me fine," Hans replied.

"Either way, you must learn to cut wood," said his father, handing him an ax. "Go, and take something to eat."

Hans wandered a short way into the forest and sat down beneath a big tree. It's too fine a day for cutting wood, he thought. And laying aside his ax, he took out his pancake and cider.

Just then Hans noticed a small sad face watching him. "Little friend, are you hungry?" asked the boy. "I have only this pancake, but it's large enough for two. And the cider is cool and sweet."

The troll bounded over, for that is who it was. "Thank you, dear boy," he said, gobbling up Hans's lunch. "Since you are so kind, I'll tell you a secret. Set your ax to this tree. You'll find something special inside it."

"Oh, no! I'm not strong enough to chop down such a tree," protested Hans.

"Not strong enough, perhaps," said the troll, "but very kind."

Then he was gone.

No sooner did Hans strike the tree with his ax than it fell with a crash. And sitting amid the upturned roots was a goose with feathers of pure gold!

"*Cwonk!*" said the goose. "Good day to you, young sir."

Hans was amazed. "A golden goose! And a talking one, at that! Why are you living inside a tree?"

"Because I was imprisoned here by a fairy witch," replied the goose. "How else could such a thing happen?"

"I don't know," Hans admitted.

"And who but a witch would dare steal me from my owner? Can you tell me that?"

"No . . . ," said Hans. "But, please, who is your owner?"

"Why, dear Princess Rosamund, of course," the goose answered. "If you return me to her, you'll be well rewarded by her father, the king."

"Return you I will," said Hans, "but I want no reward." So he tucked the goose under his arm and set out for the king's castle.

Hans had not gone far before he met two milkmaids. As he hurried by, one of them reached out to pluck a golden feather—and her hand stuck like glue to the bird's tail. "Sister!" she cried. "Pull me free! I am caught by this terrible goose!"

The second maid came running. But as soon as she touched her sister's hand, she too was held tight. The milkmaids had no choice but to follow Hans everywhere he went.

"*Cwonk!* Serves you right, my little goslings," the goose laughed.

As they continued on their way, they met Parson John. When he saw the three, the parson scolded, "Shame on you girls, chasing after a young fellow like this." He grabbed hold of the second maid's milk bucket to drag her away, but hardly had he touched it when he was forced to run after them.

"My, but you're a fine catch!" said the goose as the four tramped on.

Then the baker came by. "Wait, Parson John!" he called. "Where are you going? I've brought your afternoon crullers." He took hold of the parson's shoulder but was pulled along as well.

"There's another one!" sang the goose.

The five hurried on, one after another, and soon passed Greta the cook in her garden. "One moment, Mr. Baker," she called. "I must borrow a pound of flour for my dumplings." But when she tugged at the baker's apron, the goose cried, "Six!"

Next they met a wandering minstrel. "What's this?" he asked. "Are you playing crack the whip?" He reached to join in the fun. . . .

"Seven!" cwonked the goose. And Hans strode on, with all of them trailing behind him.

Meanwhile, Princess Rosamund was very unhappy. Day and night she sat at her window, longing for the return of her beautiful golden goose.

The king grieved to see his daughter so sad and proclaimed that whoever could make her smile might have her hand in marriage.

But no one could, and Rosamund grew more and more sad.

Gazing from her window that afternoon, the princess saw something strange—a line of people zigzagging willy-nilly across the distant fields.

How odd, thought Rosamund. Could it be a parade? She looked harder. There were seven in all, marching this way and that, one behind the other.

"Well, that's the silliest thing I've ever seen!" The sad princess giggled in spite of herself. Then she began to laugh. "My goodness, they're all stuck together!" And Rosamund laughed and laughed until she nearly fell out of her window.

Hearing her, the golden goose flew up from Hans's arms. The magic spell was broken, and the seven marchers tumbled apart.

Princess Rosamund was so happy that her goose had come home! The king sent for Hans to ask if he wished to marry his daughter—when he was older, of course.

"If the princess will have me," said Hans.

"She will," replied Rosamund, smiling.

When they grew up, they had a wonderful wedding. Parson John presided. Greta the cook prepared a feast. Mr. Baker made a cake. The minstrel sang. The two milkmaids were maids of honor.

And Hans and Rosamund lived happily ever after,
with the golden goose and her many little goslings.